Jill Mercer

Trafalgar Pigeon

© Jill Mercer Oct 2005

This is the first edition of
Trafalgar Pigeon 2011,
an imprint of Seesaw Press
and the first story in the Beaky Tales series.

Book Designer: Kim Thorpe. email: studio@platinumdesign.biz
Beaky Tales logo designer: Neal Lankester
Editing and proofreading: Penny Wilson and Veronica Symons

Published by Seesaw Press
Printed in the UK by Geerings Print Ltd, Ashford.

ISBN 978-0-9570693-0-5

www.seesawpress.co.uk
email: seesawpress@yahoo.co.uk

INTRODUCTION

I first wrote Trafalgar Pigeon in 2005 as one of a series of short stories for the ever growing number of children of my friends and family. The story of TP was inspired by the determination of those delightful little people to walk and talk and the way their differences made them special and who they were.

Birds have always been a symbol of freedom and those with a good song like the blackbird, lark and thrush are a treat to hear, especially their song just before dawn. In our cities and towns we no longer hear so many songbirds, but if you're awake early and listen carefully you may just hear a blackbird sing. Some songbirds, in their effort to attract a mate, have even been known to imitate the ringtone of a mobile phone or use a bird box as a microphone to amplify their song.

Pigeons of a similar type to the ones you see in our big cities and those that used to congregate in Trafalgar Square were once trained in different countries to deliver letters and news across land and sea. The ancient Egyptians and Persians were the first to use carrier pigeons some 3,000 years ago and the ancient Greeks used them to take news of Olympic victories. By the 19th century pigeons were widely used as messengers in many European countries and as far afield as New Zealand, where their service was known as pigeon-grams. In Great Britain the hardy little pigeons were best known for their brave work as carrier pigeons during World War I and World War II. They could fly at great speed, making themselves difficult targets as they crossed dangerous territory from the frontline battlefields with vital information, usually tied to one of their legs. Thirty-two pigeons were awarded the Dickin Medal – a wartime medal for bravery introduced by the PDSA in 1943.

Trying to find an illustrator who can bring your characters to life in the way you have visualised them when writing the story is not easy. Several other talented illustrators offered to illustrate Trafalgar Pigeon but it was Gill Wren's humorous cartoon style that looked instantly right. With each new drawing she did it seemed to just visually capture the scene on the page. Gill's style is perfect for TP's character and I'm so glad she agreed to produce Trafalgar Pigeon with me and to work on the rest of the Beaky tales series.

If you like the story of TP and want more, then look out for Wi, Wit and Woo - the next in the Beaky tales series.

Jill Mercer

3

Trafalgar Square became the home for many unemployed City of London messenger pigeons after they held their first meeting there, back in the old days of 1840, following the introduction of the Penny Black and the extended Royal Mail.

--- --- ---

It was in the year of 1840 when Ernest, Trafalgar Pigeon's great-great-great, and more greats, grandfather first heard of the 'Penny Black', a name that made every messenger pigeon who heard its name tremble with fear.

Ernest was delivering an urgent message to Hampton Court Palace when he bumped into a doleful-looking pigeon perched on the head of a stone lion.

"What's ailing you, young pigeon?" he asked.

"Coo…" replied the young pigeon from the north of England. "I've just been told there's no work nor food for the likes of me anymore, not now our masters have The Penny Black."

"Penny Black? What type of bird is that?" enquired Ernest feeling worried, but not sure why.

"It's n'er some bird, it's some sticky thing they call a stamp. Hundreds ride in sacks on the back of steel dragons that run over fields and meadows."

--- --- ---

Word spread rapidly across the pigeon world of the great city that a meeting was to take place under the long shadow of Nelson's Column, in Trafalgar Square, at the foot of the majestic fountain.

There, hundreds of pigeons huddled together in groups to discuss their fate.

By the time the city had quietened at the end of a long noisy day, the pigeons had all agreed on one thing – their future looked bleak.

"Coo, it's the end. Us and the London Hackney Horses are all doomed," predicted one pigeon gloomily. Some brave hearts decided to leave London and look for employment in England's north and other lands, but most stayed to face a life of poverty, overcrowding and squalor.

--- --- ---

No longer fed by their old masters, food was scarce and the pigeons had to scavenge amidst the jostle of feet and barrows of Brewer Street Market. Then one day, a man who had been a keeper of messenger pigeons took pity on the hungry and bedraggled pigeons that lived in Trafalgar Square.

"Oh, you poor hungry pigeons, what have we done to you?" he exclaimed. "I will bring you food."

Every day, without fail, he would take bags of seed to feed them and they all cooed round him with gratitude. When he died, the man's descendants carried on feeding the pigeons. Generation after generation dutifully took the bags of seed to Trafalgar Square. There is no doubt that, without their compassion, the London Pigeon would have long become extinct.

--- --- ---

Trafalgar Pigeon was born in 1998 on the statue of Nelson, protected by Nelson's large brimmed hat. His brothers and sisters spent most of their time begging for more food on the ground, but TP liked to be up high where he could dream of a better life.

Every night he perched on top of Nelson's column next to his one-legged mentor, Hardy, a pigeon of considerable years from the north of England. There they perched side by side, surveying the Square and beyond, and TP would listen intently to Hardy's stories of travel and expeditions.

"Ah, yes, those were the days," Hardy would say dreamily, "there's more to life than a few seeds and a mouldy crust in your face yer know, lad."

--- --- ---

One night, Hardy looked unusually gloomy. He shook his head.

Ah, lad, it's grave news... very grave indeed. The Mayor of London wants rid of us... says we make his city untidy. Huh! This is our home. I flew down from up North with my Da when I still had down on my wings." He paused, and then continued in a defeated voice: "Won't sleep on the column tonight, lad. No, think I'll take a hop around."

The following morning TP woke early to a commotion in the Square below.

"Oh no terrible... coo... terrible... how we going to tell him... terrible... terrible."

TP looked down, saw the flattened corpse in the road and was staring in disbelief when Pinny Pigeon flew up to join him. She put a comforting wing round him while she explained:

"He went quick, luv... a bus you see. Don't know why he decided to cross the road... not with only one leg an' all. Now, don't upset yerself too much 'cos he 'ad a good life."

With tears in his eyes, TP flew down and collected a few of Hardy's feathers from the road to lie at the foot of Nelson's Column. Some of the other pigeons joined him, heads bowed, in two minutes' silence.

They gazed solemnly at the feathers until TP announced tearfully, while puffing his chest out proudly:

"I'm going to leave Trafalgar Square, just like Hardy. I'm off to discover the world and have adventures."

"Huh, coo." said Card Sharp Pigeon sarcastically. "You didn't really believe the old boy's stories, did yer? No use in daydreaming – you wanna find yourself a nice little hen and settle for a window ledge. I'm telling you there's nothing out there for the likes of you. This is it pal."

But TP was undeterred. He decided to leave the next morning.

--- --- ---

His journey was slow to start with because he had never previously flown further than Oxford Circus or higher than Nelson's column, but he soon found his wings got stronger and he could fly a greater distance without getting out of breath.

TP finally arrived at Richmond Park just before sunset and settled himself on a branch next to a pair of wood pigeons.

"Wow!" he said excitedly, expelling what breath he had left into the nearest wood pigeon's face. "Look at all these trees and green stuff. Great pad you have here... and what a garden, eh?"

Hen Wood Pigeon turned up her beak disdainfully and, in unison, both wood pigeons took a few sideward steps along the branch away from TP.

"Where are you from?" asked the male wood pigeon snootily, as he looked over TP's scruffy feathers.

"Trafalgar Square," replied TP in his best London accent. "Oh, nearly forgot... yep, never travel empty beaked. 'Ere," he said as he placed a partly chewed blackberry between them. Both wood pigeons stared at the blackberry in disbelief. Hen Wood Pigeon turned her head away from Trafalgar Pigeon.

"Oh, goodness, Gregory," she said, "it's just too much. I'm not sharing our tree with... with that thing. Don't just sit there; you're supposed to defend me. DOOO something!"

Gregory stepped aside from Hen Wood Pigeon to confront TP. He cleared his throat:

"Look here, sonny, this is a Royal Park and I know it may seem harsh, but I'm afraid you can't stay here."

TP lowered his head trying to hide the tears welling up in his eyes.

"Now take a grip, lad," fluffed Gregory. "Well, as it's getting dark, perhaps one night… but not in this tree."

"No, not in OUR tree." added Hen Wood Pigeon.

"Quite," said Gregory looking at a demoralised TP, whose beak was nearly touching his feet. "Hurmf, well, it's not your fault lad, I don't suppose those London rough necks taught you any pecking order. It's just not the done thing to try and fly above your station. Well, never mind, no harm done. You just fly along now. There…" he said and pointed a wing in the direction of a shrub. "It's not occupied, so you take that one; but just for tonight, mind."

TP was hurt by the snooty, over-bloated wood pigeons, but soon recovered his cheerfulness as he settled himself into the shrub and looked up at the stars.

"Ah, this is the life," he said, as he adjusted a few twigs to make himself more comfortable. "Gregory, huh! What kind of name's that for a bird? They can keep their big old lumpy tree.

I like this cosy shrub better anyway." He stretched his wings, blinked his eyes and drifted off to sleep.

--- --- ---

The next morning, before the sun rose, he woke with a start to the trumpeting din of a dawn chorus. Unable to get back to sleep, he decided to make an early start and headed south in the direction of Sussex. Flying higher than he had ever flown before, he was awe-struck by the scenery below.

"If you could only see me now, look, I've done it, I've done it, for us both," he said, thinking of Hardy and turning a somersault in midair.

That evening he found a Sussex barn and this time he decided to check out its occupants.

"Hump, excuse me," he said to an owl perched up on the highest beam.

The owl turned its head sideways and blinked open its eyes.

"My wings are killing me," said TP, "so is it OK if I put my beak down here tonight?"

The owl blinked its eyes again. "Terwoo. Why not? I share with bats, rats, House Martins and mice, so why not a… err… what are you?"

"A pigeon," replied TP.

"A pigeon, eh? Good. Well, to-woo, 'night pigeon," said the owl and closed its eyes.

TP looked around the barn and saw a ladder leading to a level full of hay.

"Looks comfy," he said to himself, and decided to try out a hay bed for the night. He was just drifting off into a peaceful sleep when he felt a heavy, warm fish-smelling breath on the back of his neck.

"Urrgh yuk, coo, what's that?" he screeched, nearly jumping out of his feathers.

"Don't be alarmed," purred the cat, placing one paw on TP's head and prodding TP's plump chest with a drawn claw.

TP nearly fainted when the owl swooped, dive-bombing the cat.

"Screeeech… scat cat… screech… leave him alone… screeeech."

The cat lashed out at the owl to defend itself and reluctantly had to let go of TP.

21

"Quick, fly to a beam, you stupid pigeon," called the owl.

Drama over, TP tried to quieten his breathing as he looked down at the cat that was now preoccupied with a little mouse. He looked up at Owl on the beam above with gratitude.

"Oh, thanks mate, you were brilliant... the way you did that swoop and screechy thing... you saved my life. Coo, that cat was scary; I've never seen one close up before."

"Well, you have now," said the owl firmly. "Goodnight!"

--- --- ---

In the morning, TP said farewell to Owl and continued on his way. He flew south until his wings got tired and he found another place to rest – a small copse at the foot of the South Downs. Here he stayed for two days, stretching to preen his feathers and lazing in the sun. Warm and snug in the branches of an old Oak tree in the Sussex countryside, he awoke to a vision of beauty; a white dove gracefully turned her head to look briefly at him as she flew past. TP fell instantly in love. He lost his footing in his haste to shake himself awake and fell into a thorny bush below.

"Cooo... coo, what a bird. Hey, white bird, wait for me," cooed TP, untangling himself from the bush. As he shook his feathers and took off in flight, he thought to himself: "Oh? How do I know if it's a girl bird? No, I know it is 'cos I'm sure I wouldn't be feeling like this otherwise."

He followed the dove to a dovecote nearby and started to coo-coo in an attempt to win her affections. At first, she was unresponsive and irritated by the scruffy -looking pigeon dancing round her, standing on his beak and turning somersaults.

Besides, she had another suitor and Handsome Dove was thoroughly approved of by the head of the dovecote.

Early one morning, when TP was looking particularly bedraggled, having stood outside the cote all night in the rain, Handsome Dove pushed him out of the way with his puffed up breast and started coo-cooing to the lovely lady dove the others called Love Dove. She stood at the entrance of the dovecote and although her heart gave a surprising leap when she saw the bedraggled TP, Handsome Dove was the obvious suitor.

TP left the scene, head down, demoralised and beaten. But suddenly he brightened when he heard a lark sing. The beautiful song lifted his spirits and tapping out the beat, he tried to sing along. The lark winced.

"Ovf, NO, stop it! STOP! That's terrible and you can't do a duet with me," said the lark. "You'll need some singing lessons."

TP gladly exchanged worms for lessons and within a week, he had learned a beautiful tune.

Practising his new song on the way, he went back to the dovecote, took out his sheet music and tapped his beak on the music stand like a maestro. Then burst into song. His voice soared and surrounded the dovecote and the serenade entranced all the doves inside.

"Now the owner of that song is obviously of good breeding. He could well be the one for you," said the head of the cote.

As Love Dove walked daintily to the cote door, Head Dove followed her, curious to see the songster. They were both equally astonished to discover that the song bird was TP, who stood proud with his chest puffed and head held high.

"Don't encourage him. Get back inside!" ordered Head Dove. But it was too late, for Love Dove's heart was won.

TP may have won Love Dove's affections but now he faced the hardest task of all – to persuade Head Dove to accept him into the dovecote. None of the doves were happy to allow a scruffy pigeon into their cote and Handsome Dove was outraged at losing Love Dove to such a bird.

"Coo. How could you possibly love that grey patchy scruff more than me?" whined Handsome Dove to Love Dove.

"Not to worry son," said Head Dove. "He'll never survive the tasks I'm about to give him."

Head Dove gave TP three heroic tasks to perform before he would give his consent. The first task was to fly further than any carrier pigeon to collect an Edelweiss flower from one of the mountains in the Swiss Alps.

The second task was to jump from North America's Grand Canyon blindfolded, and the third task was to bring back a tail feather from the Great White Eagle, which lived on the icy shores of Norway. Head Dove was confident these tasks were so dangerous that TP would either concede or die in the process. TP squared up to Head Dove bravely and looked him in the eye:

"Right, yep, coo, consider it done."

But TP had a big problem: he was terrified of any real heights and couldn't swim. Even on his travels he always flew quite low and never much higher than Nelson's Column and he always avoided flying over water. So he went off to consult the owl that had saved him from the cat in the barn. TP knew the owl to be wise, but Owl wasn't any help. He just told him to be sensible and to go back to Trafalgar Square.

Then TP had a brainwave and remembered the bravest bird he knew. So he flew to Scotland to find Scottish Golden Eagle, who he had once met when she had come to London to visit a cousin and had lost her way.

"Can you teach me to be brave?" he asked her.

Scottish Golden Eagle wanted to help TP get over his fear of heights and she tried everything. But his knees wouldn't stop shaking even when he was blindfolded on top of a pylon.

"Go on jump!" she told the petrified TP. "It's not high and you can fly."

But it was no good. He just couldn't do it and when Golden Eagle gave him a gentle push, he hyperventilated and nearly had a heart attack.

"Och, I'm sorry, wee pigeon," she said, taking off his blindfold and fanning him with her huge wing. "I think the owl was right… why not forget Love Dove and go back to Trafalgar Square?"

"I can't," replied TP tragically, while getting shakily to his feet. "I'd rather die."

"Ay. Well, that is likely if you decide to carry on."

TP picked up the blindfold in his beak and held it out to her.

"Go on blindfold me, I'll try again."

Golden Eagle looked at the blindfold swinging from TP's beak and had an idea.

"I know," she said, "it might be worth a try. I could try to hypnotise you into believing you're an eagle rather than a poor wee frightened pigeon. I've seen it done once by my aunt, when my cousin was afraid to take his first flight from the nest."

"OK," said TP, "I'll try anything."

Eagle was successful in hypnotising the willing pigeon, but his belief in being an eagle slightly worried her as she watched him spread his little wings to take the air current off the mountaintop. As he thanked her and said farewell, she told him she was not sure how long the hypnosis would last.

"Be careful now, wee pigeon" she warned him.

--- --- ---

He flew higher than he'd ever flown before and with ease, over land and sea. As the gulls watched TP soar, he became the talk of the shores. He found an Edelweiss flower on one of the Swiss mountaintops and held it carefully in his beak on the long, homebound journey to the dovecote. Much to the surprise and annoyance of Head Dove of the cote, TP took a bow before presenting the Edelweiss to Love Dove, who accepted it coyly.

"Hurmp, yes, well, that's enough... Well done." said Head Dove reluctantly, while silently reassuring himself that even if Pigeon managed to complete task two, he was unlikely to survive the final task.

When TP reached the Grand Canyon, he asked a Canada Goose to assist him by tying the blindfold and being a witness.

"No problem," said the Canada Goose, "...and I can do better than that, I'll snatch a photograph from one of the tourists as proof for you to take back to Head Dove."

With task two complete, he flew off in search of the Great White Eagle.

But when Trafalgar Pigeon was confronted with the Great White Eagle, the hypnosis started to wear off and his nerve left him just as he held up his claw to challenge Great White Eagle to a duel. The Great White Eagle looked down at the little pigeon and cawed an ear-shattering laugh.

"You're kidding me, right?" he bellowed. "Haw, haw, that's the funniest thing ever… I'm laughing… can't believe it… I'm actually laughing. Wow, little pigeon, you're brilliant," said Great White Eagle, slapping his head with his wing. "I've been depressed for weeks and… haw, haw… you've just cured me. I'd even give you a peck on the beak if I was that way inclined."

TP, who had broken out into a sweat and just managed to stop himself from fainting, backed along the cliff top away from the huge, guffawing bird "Oh… right, well…any time… I'm glad you liked my joke and it's a pleasure to be of help."

The Great White Eagle patted TP on his head with a great white wing and said genially:

"Is there anything I can do for you little pigeon?"

"Erm, well", replied TP, feeling more confident and taking a step forward, "as a matter of fact, there is… erm… I don't suppose you have a spare tail feather lying around do you?" He went on to explain his situation and Great White Eagle, himself a romantic, was happy to oblige.

--- --- ---

It was two weeks or more before TP returned to the dovecote and produced a photograph of him falling blindfolded from the Grand Canyon. He laid it at Head Dove's feet. Then, to astonished gasps and coos from the doves around him, he did a triumphant beak stand and shook his tail feathers before proudly presenting to his true Love Dove one of Great White Eagle's tail feathers.

She held open her wings and, with eyes closed, gave TP a gentle peck. Handsome Dove, defeated, left with his head bowed while Head Dove conceded with reluctance.

"Well, with much regret, I give my consent to you, a scruffy pigeon, and our own Love Dove, to take each other by the wing and enter the dovecote together," he announced gravely while holding the dovecote door open.

"No need to get your beak in a twist, dad," said TP, giving Head Dove a friendly nudge and a wink. "Too stuffy in there for me."

"Yes," interrupted Love Dove, "we've talked things over and I too would like to spread my wings. So we've decided to live in Greenwich Park in London."

"Yeh," said TP enthusiastically. "Great space to bring up chicks and we're going to give singing lessons for extra berries."

Head Dove, for once, was speechless and others cooed quietly in awe.

"You will be so welcome to visit anytime," said Love Dove in a comforting voice to one of her tearful sisters.

"Yep, our door will always be open," concluded Trafalgar Pigeon wryly.

They looked at each other affectionately, cooed their farewells and took off majestically into a clear blue sky . . .

Trafalgar Pigeon

Author : Jill Mercer
Illustrations : Gill Wren

Published by Seesaw Press
www.seesawpress.co.uk
email: seesawpress@yahoo.co.uk

Look out for future stories in
the Beaky Tales series . . .

© Jill Mercer Oct 2005